There will be days, Brown boy

There will be days, Brown boy

poems

Alejandro Jimenez

MOUTHFEEL PRESS

MOUTHFEEL PRESS

Table of Contents

para los que nos fuimos y no hemos podido regresar;
para los que nos fuimos y regresamos a un lugar que
ya no existe, sin personas que ya no viven;
para los que nos esperan—siempre—con los brazos abiertos.

for those of us that left and have not been able to return,
for those of us that left and returned to a place
that no longer exists, with people no longer living;
for those that wait for us—always—with open arms.

"My memory will retain what is worthwhile. My memory knows
more about me than I do; it doesn't lose what deserves to be saved."

—Eduardo Hughes Galeano, *Days and Nights of Love and War*
September 3, 1940 – April 13, 2015

I worry that my memory is a weapon, Eduardo. Not that I think violent thoughts, no, but it seems that my memory keeps things that cause me both joy and pain. Land, Eduardo, I think fondly of it, but my grandfather might be dead because he fought for it. My family does not plant on the Land that made my grandmother a widow. Maybe someday I will have enough money to buy it back. Home, Eduardo, lives in a nice house in my memory. The house is wood and brick with many windows, mountains in the distance, gardens and trees abound. I look out the windows, and I have no idea where I am. Out of one window, I am with my friends, and we are playing marbles under an almond tree and butterflies float in the air. Out of another window, people like me are rounded up, put in cages — adult and little ones alike — and kept as cheap labor. I worry that my memory is only keeping things to confuse me, Eduardo. I worry that I remember too much. I am always wanting to both forget and remember. What is the English or Spanish word for that? Memory can be such a curse, wouldn't you agree? If I did not remember Home, maybe I would have no trouble focusing on things like thriving in this new land. I have watered gardens in both places, Eduardo, but different vegetables came up. Maybe my memory is not satisfied with what I remember. Perhaps it needs new things. I am not satisfied with being both from here and from there. That's too simple for me. The memory of my heart seems to only have room for one country. That may also be too simple, and it also implies the need for borders. See, Eduardo! This is where memory can be violent. Do you think that each organ and each part of our body can have its own memory? Food always tastes better back Home. My heart hurts more in this land, it is happier in that Land. My spine does not bend back in that Land. I want my skin to be transparent in this land. Questions of belonging do not bother me back Home. I am not trying to forget anything, Eduardo. I know memory will remember. I am trying to figure out why it remembers what it does, why it forgets what it does, and what is worthwhile in keeping memories that make me feel torn apart.

For the days when your belonging is questioned

Poem about immigration without. . .

using the following words or phrases or any of its variations: immigrant, "we [they] just want to work", DREAMER, border, deported, separation, ICE/Migra, immigration raid, "a better life", "living in the shadows", citizenship, papers, we are home, etc.

In the photo, I am three years old, and off camera, our dog, a black and red Doberman without a tail that we nicknamed Mocho, was still alive.

He hadn't eaten whatever made him start puking uncontrollably, which caused my grandmother to ask my uncle to put Mocho out of his misery. I stood atop the basurero as mocho's lifeless body—

now with a hole in its head—was thrown down the cliff into the river. There was a lot of trash, but Mocho was the first dead dog I had seen in it. His body stopped rolling, belly up and over time, I would watch the sun, crows, insects, and other dogs uncover the pearly white ribs hidden underneath his black fur. I would make a habit of visiting Mocho.

In the photo, I am three years old, and I am smiling at the camera. I have a knife in my hand, and I am cutting into the cake, but I don't remember eating. Off camera, the mandarina tree has not been cut down, and the lemon tree is planted in a bucket. It was August; it was cloudy and muggy that day. My grandmother threw water on the dirt floor to keep the dust from rising

                                  [onto my cake, of course].

In the photo, I am [mostly] complete. I've not met grief. It was the first time I met my mother   [well, my first memory of her anyway].

In the photo, I am wearing an all-blue outfit   [even then, I disliked wearing all one color]. I remember feeling blue. I remember running into the bedroom and hiding under the bed, and

my mother tried to console me, but she was a stranger back then. I would not remember her until I was eight years old, and I was standing on carpeted floors, and the scent in the house was new   [even the birdsongs needed translating].

I felt like Mocho: belly-up, unable to shoo away the insects coming to nibble on my flesh.

Green Card

I was asleep when I crossed into this country for the first time. I remember only the anticipation. Then—10 years later—I was wide-eyed, staring into my second crossing. I was more angry than excited during my green card interview. The immigration officer had her lunch on top of my paperwork, and my mother prayed silently. The officer chewed loudly, and it annoyed me.

The chewing—so mundane and ordinary, my heart heavy and immensely void of feeling. The office was barren, but the view of the Willamette River made up for it. If approved, it meant an end to the wait. It meant no more yearly immigration physicals, and I would not be checked for lice or made to undress and answer, *no, I do not have AIDS or HIV.*

[*Can I get it from masturbating? I always wanted to ask that.*]

My mother prayed nervously in a whisper. Immigrants often confuse this country for God. *Legal status* is the closest to God some of us will ever be. The officer, in my mother's eyes, was St. Peter. I wanted to answer sufficiently enough so the pearly gates would open, and I would walk out of the office with a sliver of heaven that could easily fit in my wallet.

On paper, I am a case number. If approved, I would be given an *Alien Number.* If approved, I would have to carry a card with my picture and *Alien Number* on it at all times. I could more easily get in debt with an *Alien Number.* The system would acknowledge me, even if the number stripped me of my humanness. How we negotiate our humanity in this country is a funeral, and I am no good at praying.

The only questions I remember from the interview: Are you a communist? Are you a prostitute? Are you a drunk? I answered no to all. But I wanted to say: *I like to break bread with people, so I am communal. Right now, I am selling myself to you. I do not know what the feeling of being drunk is, but I imagine it feels like you are not in control of your own body.*

We walked out, my mother thanking God and his messenger,
and me, staring into the officer's eyes—this crossing

I will remember.

You're Mexican

After Fatimah Asghar

You're Mexican until you go to a white college. Then you are Latino/a/@/x. His panic. Her panic. Everyone's panic! They just want to tell you about the time they visited Costa Rica, Puerto Rico, or Ecuador. You let them know *that that's not Mexico. What's the difference? They speak Spanish, too!* [insert white teeth smiling, lips like nooses waiting to tighten around a neck if challenged]. They just want to tell you stories about some resort manicured for their lily-pink bodies where the water is filtered and purified before it touches their skin, and the sand on the beach is made of stars. It is lukewarm on their feet, and the seashells are individually polished every night and thrown on the ground before they can order a *Sir-Bay-Zah.*

> You're Mexican until they find out you got papers a couple of months before starting college. Then, you are their shot at redemption. You are a ticket to ease their white guilt. *You are proof that the system is not broken, Alex!* You're Mexican until they discover you grew up as a farmworker. Then, you are a Yelp review representative and all they want to know is *where the best 'you pick it' farm is located.* You're Mexican until you make your way toward the dinner table, and one of them loudly says, *here comes the beaner,* and they all laugh and one of them tries to have your back: *he's not that much of a beaner.* They laugh. You sit with them and eat your dinner anyway because this is the price of the American dream. They will joke about running away to Canada if an election threatens their liberal lifestyle.

> > You're Mexican until you start calling yourself—Brown. Until you stop laughing at their jokes. Then, you are *angry. Then, you are like the rest of them.* You're Mexican until you say *no human being is illegal.* Until you say *borders are just an idea we decide(d) to build.* Then, *you are ungrateful!* Then, *why are you here?*

Because.
We have planted and harvested the food on your plate.
We deserve to eat it   too.

My First Halloween in College

I dressed up as a *Mexican.*

And like any good [wannabe] white boy, I drove
with my white friends to the second-hand store
to buy an outfit.

I bought a straw sombrero with a purple and pink brim.
I bought a black vest with different colored stripes and pockets
that would rest against my chest.

Hey! You could put a small bottle of tequila in a pocket,
my white friend said.
Yea, yea, yea! That's a [racist] good idea!

I bought a pair of green neon shorts that stopped before reaching my ankles.
I wanted to look like a piñata or something easy to break. Something
whose pieces could be swept away.

Brown at a predominately white institution
is where you earn the stripes of the American Dream,
is where the border comes to laugh in your face,
is the price of "making it"
is where you do anything to walk across that stage in May.

America, what ugly chameleons you make of us.

[**beaner**]

When you say it, mean it.
Your tongue must not stumble.
Wrap your whole mouth around it.

[beaner]

Just like that. With all the jitters
of a first kiss, with all the awkwardness
of holding hands for the first time.

[beaner]

Just like that. You must feel dirty, no?
All those dying bodies flat on your lips
in nice neat rows of corn, and the wind

[beaner]

carrying their moans to the back of your throat
like a coyote guides brown bodies
into the desert, into death. There must be

[beaner]

a tombstone where your Adam's apple is.
All that praying to your white God and
still you spit on my ribs He made

[beaner]

from your body. You must not like your own reflection.
There must be bullets where your teeth are.
What privilege, murdering,

[beaner]

knowing you got those borders
and those politicians and all those
courts and all the constitution protecting you.

[beaner]

If you are going to gnaw on my throat,
say it so that at least it sounds worthwhile.
Even when you think it.

[   ]

Mean it then, too

Museo

At the Museo de Antropología in Mexico City
the two European tourists *uh!* and *ah!*
while the brown tour guide pronounces
the word *metate*   very   slowly
as if counting
the money he will
be tipped
with his tongue.

I cannot blame him for talking about us
as if we no longer exist.
We are all surviving one way or another.
I guess I am bothered that we kill a little bit
of ourselves each time we deny
our existence.

Survival, like genocide, also means death.

Still, My First Halloween in College

An Asian student hosted a
"Most Offensive Halloween Party"
where he dressed as Hitler.

A brown woman wore a dress
covered in blood with a sign that read,
"raped Indian".

They were both asked to apologize.

The following fall during a school-wide talent show,
in my predominantly white institution,
a white student sings every N-word, every epithet
of Dr. Dre's "B*tches Ain't Shit".

For them
we have campus-wide conversations
about oppression and race.
Our student fees pay for Tim Wise

to visit our campus and give a lecture
on White privilege.
They ask us [students of color] if we feel better.

Wyoming

The clouds part, and the blue sky rests high above us.
    The birds harmonize with the wind.

The dust rises from the dirt road we drive on,
    finds a home on the paint job of our Acura.

We are west of Laramie and
    I think about Matthew Shepard.

If the White boys made a ghost
    out of one that looks like them. . .

I imagine running toward the hills, flanking the sides
    of the road where a herd of cows graze in the middle.

I ease on the gas, and the earth thanks me.
    There is a pick-up truck across the herd.

Two bodies in it are wearing camo. The grand reaper cannot hide.
    If the prey sees it coming, it cannot be surprised.

If their set of hands, at this junction or the next, should turn
    this brown into a feast for earthworms,

I pray that it be fast. No Shepard.
    I do not want to gift them the trickle of my breath.

The clouds darken, and raindrops thunder down,
    cows move out of the way.

I drive fast, and the bikes on the bike rack rattle,
    and snakes, be warned.

I stare into the rearview mirror; just in case, I say,
    This road is beautiful; I'd like to run many, many miles on it.

Placing her hand to massage my neck
    to ease the tension,

my girlfriend whispers, *You would*, and looks
    into her side mirror, *You would.*

American Enough

I never meant to be *this* American.
Always kept apple pie away from my mouth.
I learned English. I stood for the Pledge.
I have purposely mispronounced my own name.

I wanted to be a ghost—there, but not always seen.
I wanted to be American *enough* so I could vacation
on foreign beaches so I could be deemed beautiful
without having to second guess my body,
and I would not have to bite my tongue, and my anthem
would end with my people cheering instead
of exit wounds in their backs.

                                        But I have sinned.

I have become *too* American.
My teeth are filled with cavities
from every sugary star I have ingested.

                                        Depression—
                                        or whatever you call this shit—
                                        is beyond patriotic.

Now, I have no homeland
and therapy on Thursdays.

For the days when all you want is to return home

Dreams

There is the one about seeds. My grandmother places them before me.
My hometown is burning. Piles of bodies. Pyramids we did not intend to build.
    There is the one where I am running out of the bull-riding ring, bulls
chasing after me, exhaling red steam from their noses that turn into arrows.
I turn the corner, and there is a labyrinth of snakes. The snakes are thick,
dark green, and hang from trees. I cannot tell where one ends and the other
begins. One looks at me, see, you are home. I hang, monkey-bar style, from
a branch. I hiss at the bulls. They run, shivering in fear.
      There is the one where I am flying in the clouds. I am afraid of
heights, so I land on the ground but do not know what land I stand
on. I look for anything familiar. Everything is dark. There is laughter
in the distance. I walk towards it.

Not dreaming.	I sit in the backseat of a car, waiting our turn to cross into the US from Tijuana. My name has changed from *Alejandro* to that of some citizen boy I resemble somewhat, whose birth certificate we use to get me across. The coyote, who is my uncle, tells me to fall asleep. *You speak no English! They will question you if you are awake! We cannot get caught!* I fall asleep and wake under a neon sign. My aunt wraps me in a green blanket. She consoles me by caressing my forehead. I fall back asleep and wake up in a strange house with carpeted floors. My mother is hugging me, and she is crying. I feel empty, so I cry, too.
Not dreaming.	I sit across from blue-eyed Matthew, who is speaking English to me. I am in third grade and have been here for a few months. He is getting red in the face. I know no words to ask why. Resting on the table between us is a board with black and red squares. I want to play checkers. He pulls out a chess piece. I place the checkers down. He pushes them away, places his tall pieces down. I say *no*. He says *yes*. We go back and forth. *Yes. No. Yes!* No! I am confused. He gets up and leaves. I place the checkers on the board. I sit alone.
Not dreaming.	I sit on the couch staring out the window. Aside from my family and bills, there is nothing I can call my own out there.

In my land

the earth smells like skin after a swim in the river,
        there are no more sins, and all is forgiven.
        The dirt is brown, and you want to eat it when it rains.
        This land will keep me in its mouth until my blood
        blooms into a field of hibiscus flowers.
        Don't call it *reincarnation*; call it— *harvest.*

the wind rides horseback along the seams of cerros and
        makes green fields moan with pain and pleasure.
        It carries the sound of gunshots that made my grandfather
        choke on his own blood. My grandmother is La Llorona,
        weeping, but no one sees her. At night, she will tell you
        a story about heartbreak. The wind carries that, too.

the river is a contradiction. My grandmother would wash clothes in it.
        The animals drink from it. The crops feed from it. My uncles would drink
        beer next to it, swim in it, washing their sins. At times, our town would
        get woken by wailing mothers scolding the river for dragging their sons
        downstream and returning them with bloodied faces and eyes that would
        not shut.

the cemetery is a flowerbed where we sit to retell our favorite stories.
        My great-grandmother is buried here. She flung chickens from their neck,
        and *poof!* A stew was born. She mixed sugarcane alcohol with honey and
        spoon-fed it to me. And *poof!* My fear was gone. Ask me about Mexican
        Independence Day, and I will tell you about the time she left her husband
        and bought a herd of goats.

I am often asked where I am from. I pronounce the name of my land slowly:
                                                                Co li ma.
        They ask me to show them on a map. Instead, I tell them that a harvest in
        my land is a unified hymn, and fields of green and brown hands are the
        only God [or Creator] I have ever believed in.

                    Every Ash Wednesday, wherever I stand,
                    I take a fistful of dirt
                    and rub it
                    on my forehead.

                    I repent   for leaving.

Primavera

When the butterflies flew toward the river at the bottom of the canyon, I would stand in the middle of the street and stick my arms out. *If I don't move, they will land on me,* I'd think. My friends would laugh and adults would call me crazy. Butterflies were a season in my town, and I wanted an April to bloom in.

I would run up and down the street surrounded by the yellows, the oranges, the lightest and brightest greens. It seemed I could hear their flapping wings turn the road into a roaring river, but it was the laughter coming from my friends. I'd run, trying to catch those butterfly wings. They seemed to tease me. They would fly close and flutter higher and higher and higher. I would jump and fall to the ground with sweat on my forehead, and the sky, too, wanted to cup its hands and catch the lightest and brightest of greens.

I was four or five years old when I began understanding how a seed became a plant. *Put the seed in the dirt; it will rain, and the sun will give it light, and we will pick corn in a few months,* my uncle would say. My stubby little hands would tenderly place the seed in the ground and pat down the soil like only a child can. I thought anything that went into the ground was a seed. That it would eventually come back to life.

I did not understand grief then.

I was four or five when I first saw a casket lowered to the ground. The sun was hot and hung high in the sky. It was the rainy season. Someone, maybe a mother, a lover, or father, wept so much they had to sit in the shade, and the air fanned to their lungs. I did not think much about this because, later in our town, someone had a baby. This was how I understood life: you put something in the ground, add water, give it sun, and soon you'll have something to bring joy again.

When I finally caught a butterfly, its wings tickled my palms, and I giggled. My friends asked me to show it to them. The butterfly almost escaped when I opened my hands the tiniest bit. We agreed that it was best to put it in a plastic bag so we could take turns marveling at it. Eventually, the butterfly stopped trying to escape, and the edges of its wings looked like a mountain range.

I dug a hole beside the lemon tree in my grandmother's backyard. I removed the rocks and softened the earth with my fingers. Once deep enough, I grabbed the lifeless butterfly from the bag and placed it in the hole. I patted the dirt with my stubby little hands. From the leftover soil, I built a wall around it. I made it thick enough so the water would not escape. I figured a butterfly plant would grow in a few months, just like my uncle had explained.

Even in winter, I'd have an April to bloom in.

First Time Experiencing Emptiness

I am six years old, and my grandmother is holding my hand.
I look up at her and she smiles.
I look out the window and see people waving the bus down.
The driver honks the horn, and a line forms at the corner.
There is giggling and hugging.
It is a summer sunset over my town.
It is Sunday, and people are sweeping, gossiping, and drinking at the corner.
My friends run across the street, and I cannot wait to join them.
Piles of leaves are being burned in the middle of the street.
The smoke seems to cleanse all of us.
There is a sweetness in the air, and I can hear the church bells at a distance.

When the bus stops, I look at my grandmother and out the window again. She
smiles as if holding the sun between her teeth.
She hugs me, and I cry.
I feel an emptiness inside of me,
                    deeper than the river at the bottom of the canyon.
The hollow of my chest feels like the hollow of the trees I climbed with friends,
                    but there is no laughter.

I don't know what I lost that Sunday or why I lost it.
I just know that returning always feels like I am leaving.

There Was My Home

One time
I built a fort inside the abandoned pigsty
in my grandmother's backyard—there,
I sang loudly and grieved
when the cardboard roof
on her house was replaced with cement.

I ran from my grandmother to
my great-grandmother's house once.
Upon entering, my great-grandmother
stood with a belt that bent me to my knees
and made me pray for mouthing off
to her daughter. Kneeled in front of her
mud stove and metate
my hands clasped together lightly
resting on my chest, I washed
myself of the sin I had committed.

Before I left
I planted the seeds
from the orange I was eating
at the edge of the lemon tree's shadow

After arriving here
I walked into a field of fruit trees
and lay in the tall grass that covered
my small brown body—there,
I stared at the clouds.
They were not as beautiful as the ones
back home, but they made me smile.

One time
I made a human figure
out of grass and sticks
I placed it on the trunk of a fruit tree
right where the branches begin to split
each at its own pace and direction
like a sun emerging from the ground.

If this nostalgia should crucify me, I thought,
let me wake up somewhere I am willing to leave.

In my second October here
I climbed to the top of a walnut tree
and found a nut still covered
in its green layer. I bit it
leaving my teeth printed on it
and placed it back where I had found it—there,
I wanted the rain to drip into
my mouth & make a river
out of me

flow, I said, flow on
& on & on & on
wash this new—and old—country out of me

take me

to where my body belongs.

Sometimes a Conversation is a Poem

I ask the Lyft driver taking me from the Oakland Airport to downtown Oakland:
where are you from?

        Me?   Syria.

When did you come here?

        Me?   Sorry.   Little English. 6 years.   I am old
        Haha!   my country   blood blood now.
        You   Indian, my friend?

No. Mexican.

        Oh.   This California. Mexico? Long time. Ago? Yes?

Yes. It was. Long time ago. Do you miss your country?

        My country   beautiful when me   boy.   Blood blood now.
          Sorry   little English   haha!

Yes. My country blood blood now, too. Our countries are beautiful.

        Yes   beautiful. Yes,   nice friend.   You   sorry
        little English   feel   good haha!   in my heart.
        Yes! You. Feel. Good. In my heart!

Gracias.

        What you say?

Gracias is—thank you. You feel good in my heart, too!

        Shukran, my friend, shukran.

What did you say?

        Gracias, my friend, gracias.

Bull Rider

In my town, children are told their fate by men drinking caguamas on a street corner.

Flocks of us jumping, running, and laughing down the street like butterflies in April—this is what international policy cannot monetize, what capitalism cannot destroy. The men are friends and family, so we greet them and ask if they need a mandado—our attempt at buying more beer for them and getting a small tip for sweets. Instead, they invite us to sit down and offer us a drink of beer [holy water is a matter of perspective]. Some of us take the offer. *You are not old enough!* They say, bursting into laughter and swigging their beer.

The men sit on the corner drinking after a day's work in the campo or a Saturday afternoon to recount stories so that the day will not be forgotten. So that the sun knows we are thankful for its rising and setting. In my town, the corner is abundance.

The eldest of the men stretches their index finger at one of us, *ese va a salir bueno para la pisca.* Meaning—they got good hands. The land will recognize those hands. Those hands will seduce and make it fertile for us to grow crops and eat. There is no talk about kings or royalty here. If you can work the land, you are as good as gold. He will stay.

Y ese, he points again, *¡va a hacer bien noviero!* Masculinity starts like that—an idea. He is destined to jump from bed to bed, leaving a trail of used women and an unsatisfied heart. We taunt him. He is the shy one. We all think he is gay. He never tells us otherwise. We love him. He might leave.

Este será...albañil, and the older man's face is somber, his index finger seems guilty for pointing. The other men glaze over with loss; we can almost hear the silent breath. We gently smile with sadness. We know that when he begins to build a city, he will not return. He will move away and leave us.

This happens often in my town. Those who find stability elsewhere do not return. We do not blame them. In my town, we are all trying to stay.

For my long legs that curve out at the knees. For my lanky frame resembling a rag doll. For my long spine, flexible like a copper coil, *este ¡sera un jinetazo!* A bull rider. The older man's eyes open wide, and they sparkle. He takes a long swig from his beer and others seem to make a toast at my fortune. I am the least adventurous of the group. The one that leaves before the dark is pitch. The one asking questions about how things come to be. If the Gods are right, my body will fill with muscle, my upper lip will have a mustache, and my chest will resemble a hill. This is how masculinity is upheld—the want to fill my role, oh, so desperately. Jinete means I am good as gold, too. Jinete means I will come and go often from my town. I will have many lives. I will need to learn how to seduce the land with my hands, for I will need its blessing to tame the beasts that roam it. I will leave and follow the fiestas of every neighboring town. I will find my way to the bull-riding ring and will be recognized. I will build a cathedral of followers. I will stand at the ring's center and be applauded. Nowhere will feel like home.

/ /

Juan was a jinete in our town. Brown like earth after rain. Hair that seemed to trap the wind and turn it dark. He buttoned his shirt only halfway up his chest, so we all saw his pectoral muscles flex bulls into submission when he rode them.

El Charro had the longest horns of any bull I had ever seen. I was convinced that if I stood on its head, the horns would still be longer than my six-year-old body. He was gray with a dark stripe running down his entire back to the tip of his tail. He was the goliath of our town. No jinete could ever stay on El Charro long enough to claim he won. I saw him knock riders off him with his horns. Bodies like rags would land on the dirt floor, and El Charro would dance on top of them.

It was May, the time of the fiestas in my town, when Juan conquered El Charro.

El Charro jumped and jumped. He vigorously swung his head back, trying to hit Juan with his horns. Juan dodged and dodged while grinding his teeth; the sweat reflected the sun off his exposed chest. When El Charro stopped jumping, we threw our hands up and chanted as if we were on top. My uncles threw their hats in the air, and La Banda played loudly, making us happy. Juan jumped off El Charro, ran towards the center of the bull riding ring, and took a bow.

That's when I wanted to be a bull rider.

/ /

There are various ways to ride a bull:

I. Legs wrapped around the bull's body, and both hands holding onto the rope tied around the bull's torso.

II. Same as the first, but one hand up in the air.

III. Same as first, but both hands up in the air.

IV. Same as first, with any variation of second or third options, but the rider's legs are placed at about a 45-degree angle towards the bull's chest; we call this al pecho— to the chest.

/ /

When bull riding, you should lean forward when the bull jumps. When the bull is about to land, you should lean back as if trying to lay on its back.

A rider always wears boots and their choice of spurs—the hooked ones dig into the bull's skin, or the round ones jab into the bull's sides but do not dig into the skin. In my town, real bull riders do not wear spurs.

I wanted to ride bulls with no spurs, legs to the chest with both hands on the rope, wearing white or red boots, blue Levi jeans, a solid-burgundy-colored shirt buttoned up only half-way, and a cream-colored cowboy hat with a peacock feather in it.

/ /

I stopped wanting to be a bull rider when I saw Orlando, the best-looking guy from our town, get half his face peeled off by El Charro's claw. We all gasped when it happened. His mother screamed, and everyone inside the riding ring rushed to El Charro to get it to stop dancing on top of Orlando. We thought his head was smashed, made of pulp with the dirt. His mother was weeping and negotiating with God. The birds were flying low. He got up and walked off the ring. We all clapped. El Charro was roped and held to the ground.

//

I have not seen Orlando since the day he got his face peeled off. People in my town say he hides in his house and rarely comes out. Juan is a drunk now. When I saw him a few years ago, he was dragging himself on the ground, as if something was chasing him, even though I couldn't see anything. El Charro is buried somewhere in the mountains near our town. The owner did not say where, fearing people might try to steal El Charro's horns.

//

As the older man on the corner predicted, I was unsure if I was meant to be a bull rider. I left my town before I was old enough to try to prove anything to anybody. I have not been to the fiestas in my town in over 25 years. Often, I contemplate the person I am becoming, where I want to be buried, and what parts of me would be worth stealing. Today, I am weary of the vulnerability I've carried thus far. Most days, nowhere feels like home, and I constantly marvel at how emptiness weighs heavy. I haven't broken many hearts, but I am tending to the one I've hurt many times. I haven't ridden a bull in my life, but still, I am afraid to end up like Juan and Orlando. Scared and hiding from shadows only I see.

Prayers

I don't pray with my hands clasped together as if holding air. These legs are the pews I stand on to believe in something higher. Sunday morning church means 13 or 20-mile runs. I listen to birdsongs for two hours, and trees wave at me as I pass by. My mother used to nibble on these feet of mine. Now, I cannot tell where my feet end and the ground begins. My mother does not understand why I run so much. Says I am too skinny to run. Says I should eat more caldo. Says I will faint on the trail. Sometimes—when I am tired during my run—I open my mouth to taste the sun. I am eating, even when I am full of prayers.

Cerro El Quemado

The offerings are placed on the south side of the mountain—

multi-colored ojos de dios, Mexican pesos—old and new ones,
handkerchiefs with colorful embroidered images of the Virgin Mary on them,
precious stones, bananas, granola bars, turkey feathers, human hair,
a pair of horns on top of a cactus, clay bowls, ash, and smoke edged onto rocks.

The *Wixárika* built a shrine here—

four uneven cement walls with a roof and
a gate that keeps prayers in place and
sticky fingers away.

In this shrine sits a sacred offering—

a painting detailing corn, peyote,
a deer running or walking, bow and arrows,
streams of water, and the sun.

Here—
the smell of burnt deer blood is incense
the mountain buries its tongue into the clouds
this makes the air swirl with jealousy
the sun shines and it rains in the town below

Here—
where the sun was born and blood gave fire its color.

Here is my offering—
the tears that swelled my eyes while looking at the valley below.
Take my eyes, sew them onto the sun. Take my tears and quench
the thirsty fire.

My offering—
the bag of pinole I've carried for all those miles.
The corn—what I am made of. The canela—the color of my skin.

Sometimes, fire burns brown.

Your bones are made of memory

but sometimes they are fire. Other times, there
are two decaying bodies where your femurs should be.

Especially in the mornings, your bones are
an old piano collecting dust, and there is

a dead hummingbird where your sternum
should be. Your ribs are steps leading towards

a pile of ash where your jaw should be,
your teeth are missing, you cannot chew,

and you feel you are dying of hunger. You worry
that fanning a fire will only ignite the dry

parts of you. After all, it is the dry grass that burns
the forest—the lightning is just a scapegoat.

If your bones are made of memory. What of the
bone marrow? Why is it buried so deep in you?

What memory is it trying to keep from you?

On the days I am tired of humanizing myself
I want to make a straw from a blade of grass,

puncture a hole into my pelvis and suck the
marrow into my mouth.

Go somewhere where I can eat [and remember] in peace.

For the days when you forget who you come from

How the Women in My Family Dance—in 4 Generations

Abuela Esperanza—

Imagine rows of corn, their long green leaves swaying to the rhythm of the wind. Imagine the sound they make when brushing against each other like weary waves relieved to find a resting place. Imagine the birds chirping. The crickets at night— a well-orchestrated symphony all of us know and enjoy. That calmness. That safety.

That's how I felt watching my great-grandmother dance!

She was a temple with swift legs, a good harvest season, and rain when needed. She lifted her skirt past her knees when the drums and trumpets sounded. Her feet stomped the floor one after another as if proclaiming:

This is my land. This has always been my land! And this, this is how you dance!

Her eyes fixated on the ritual, the feather-like movements of her hands. The same hands she used to hold herself up as a single mother, to till the land, and cook for an army of campesinos three times a day, seven days a week—the same hands she used to raise grandchildren and great-grandchildren like me. Those hands taught me how necessary it was to hold onto the things we cannot live without.

When the arthritis came, locking her knuckles, she did not complain about being unable to make tortillas or cook. She complained because it kept her from dancing.

And when she danced. People would point and say *Look! Esperanza is dancing! Look!*

And she knew	and showed off	and laughed.
The closest	I ever got to seeing her cry	was when she danced.

When she died, I like to imagine the hundreds of people who flocked into her tiny home from our neighboring mountain towns to pay their last respects were trying to catch one last glimpse of her dancing, while the candles surrounding her death bed were the fire to light her new shimmy. Those in attendance did not want to miss it.

There is a story I want to ask about
        but my great-grandmother's casket is hollow now.

The earthworms and field mice
        are full of words. I want her to feed me.

The earth holds everything I want my great-grandmother to teach me;
        now, I dig my hands in the dirt, hoping to feel hers.

'ama Adela—

My grandmother's dance is a slow rumble. Slowly picking up speed with every twist,
                              with every guitar strum, getting louder and louder.

She is patient with her steps. She is not as flamboyant as her mother. She doesn't
stomp the floor when she dances. She doesn't yell or swing her arms out of control.

I like how my grandmother dances. She knows there is power
in tranquility and patience in each step.

She usually cries when she dances, and I can never tell if they're tears
of joy   or sorrow.

She doesn't like attention when she dances.

Instead, she invites everybody to dance. She wants to camouflage herself
among the dancing bodies.

And we all join. And we all laugh and chant loudly.

        Amid all this,
        she steps out of the crowd,
        sits back and watches what she created.

I mean this in its entirety—poetry aside. I do not pray much. I don't believe in God,
        but seeing the grace of my grandmother's dance, I know there is
        something bigger than me. She has seen it. I know she has. So when she
        extends her hand for me to dance, I take it. I ask her to spin me. I ask her
        to take me to this higher being. I ask her to spin, twist, bend, dip, and
        throw me up in the air like rice on a wedding day, and she laughs,

calls me crazy, asks me what I am talking about, and hugs me. I feel her tears land
on my neck,   and at that moment, I realize   she is
                                                            the higher being
                                                            that I believe in.

Where do you think the rain comes from? She asks.

Where do YOU think it comes from? I counter.

Maybe from the clouds or the sky.

And we both giggle.

I squeeze her forearm, and we both agree that
it would be nice if it rained so it would cool down,
and we could eat bolillo with canela.

*I don't know if the rain comes from the sky
or if the clouds stop by a waterfall to drink
but it is raining,* she says, while shooing
the dog away   she doesn't want it
to get wet.

She leaves to turn on the canela.

The lady selling bread will be along soon.

'ama Lourdes—

My mother was dancing so fast one time that she fell.
          Her feet could not keep up with her happiness,
          so they asked her to slow down.
My mother dances like my great-grandmother,
          with the urgency of a revolt waiting
          at the brim of her feet.
She dances with the same audacity as when she crossed the border,
          as if nothing could stop her to getting where she is going,
          ask El Río Grande if she let walls get in her way.
She is an immaculate sight—dancing, an alchemist,
          turning a dance floor into her home.

When my mother dances, her feet land so hard on the floor that I know my great-grandmother is rattling the bottom of her casket with her feet, proclaiming, *That's the girl I raised!*

When my mother dances, she is a whole-body mantra. Too joyous for her tongue to be silenced. She opens her mouth, points it towards heaven, and yells. Opens her arms, inviting musicians to play faster. Cries again, tucks her hair behind her ear, bites her lip, and blesses the ground with her presence.

My mother has worked and toiled since she was a little girl. She hasn't had many days off.

Except for the day after my cousin's quinceañera, she woke up and complained of pain. She said, *my feet. They hurt from dancing. I will rest today.*

She sat on a chair, ice water in a cup, sipping and laughing about the night before, saying that it was such a shame La Banda had stopped playing at three in the morning.

The happiest I've seen my mother:

          She got up after falling.
          Dusted herself. Laughed. Grabbed one of her friends
          by the arm and   continued dancing
                                             without missing a beat.

My mother says—I love you—in the most beautiful ways:

¿Mijo, ya comistes?
Te hecho unas tortillas si quieres.

Mijo, nada más te llamaba para ver como estabas.

Mijo, ya sabes que tu mamá siempre te apoya.

Concéntrate en lo tuyo y escribe y saca tus
libros y poesía y no te detengas.

Ay, mi chiquillo tan inteligente y lindo y guapo.

Eres un orgullo. Desde chiquito dije,
él sera alguien especial.

Solamente si te viera tu abuelo.

Mijo, voy a rezar para que todo salga bien.

¡Échale ganas!

Mijo—

There is something about the women in my family and how they dance.
> How they look like a paintbrush stroking space, painting the room with
> laughter.

There is something about the women in my family and how they dance.
> How it seems as if they dance a little bit longer, a little bit faster, swaying
> their hips a little bit wider, how they unleash the revolution we so much
> romanticize—and need.

There is something about the women in my family and how they dance.
> How they are taking our narrative, giving it new meaning.

Like when they dance, we are not all tragedy. We are not all death and murder.
We do not have to bury caskets stuffed with our bodies and pretend they are seeds
anymore.

When they dance—
> We remember we are an open border of untamed Brown joy. Like, despite all
> the odds against us, we still dance. We still celebrate. For what is life without
> laughter? Why continue to fight if we do not celebrate our victories?

> Like every day we awake is a gift.
> Like every word I write is a musical note.
> Like we are sitting in the back of a room,
> the floor is open, and the women in our lives
> are center stage   they are dancing!

And we ask them to spin us, to take us to where this higher being is—

Ask them to spin, twist, bend, dip, and throw us up in the air like rice on a
wedding day.

All while chanting   ¡baila mamá, baila! ¡baila mamá, baila!

And when they extend   their hands to us,
we take them   and we dance too.

As we cook together
I ask my mother for a recipe
& everything she says is:

Grab with your fingertips   un poquito of this,
un poquito of that,   una cucharadita of
     this and of that   no más.

So, how much is un poquito, Ama?

Pues un poquito, mijo, you'll taste it
and you'll know when it is good,
she says while flipping a sope
with one hand and stirring a pot
          with her other.

The recipe is not about the dish I wish to learn to cook.

It is about trusting in and with your body to know
          when enough   is enough.

Colosio

I remember the gun appearing from amongst the crowd. I remember people yelling, *¡Le pegaron a Colosio! ¡Le pegaron a Colosio!* I remember staring at my grandmother as she stared into the TV. Her face — somber. Her eyes — two levies unfit to hold the river fast approaching. I did not know then what I know now. My mother loved Colosio. He promised something to the campesinos. To those of us living en los cerros y los campos. He spoke about land. Back then, in 1994, my grandfather had been buried for five years. He was also murdered for speaking about cerros y egidos y derechos a la tierra. Colosio and my grandfather looked alike. Both were fair-skinned Mexicans with thick black mustaches, fat from all the kisses they received from lovers. Their hair seemed to trap the air, turning it black on their head. Back then, my grandmother murmured the names of saints while the people on the TV screamed and scrambled, trying to keep the blood from leaving Colosio's body. Trying to keep the blood from making the ground blush red with embarrassment at what its children had done to each other. My grandmother wiped her tears, made the sign of the cross over the screen, and did what she always did when things around us seemed to crumble — she swept the dirt floor, sprinkled water on it to keep the wind from taking whatever remained, whatever scent, whatever blood of my grandfather the dust still held.

Coyote Bite

My mother has a scar on her right thigh.

> *That's where the coyote bit me,* she would tell my brother and me
> as she tucked us in bed.

Truth is:

my mother crossed the border over the cerro at night. The barbed-wire fence that divided Mexico and U.S. — the fence that kept her from reaching God — the fence that bit her.

> La migra was coming and the coyote was rushing everyone to run.
America pulled its teeth,   or was it Mexico?
> and bit my mother.

A price of sorts.

                            They say, Christ gave of his body for our sins.
My mother gave of her body   for her sin.

I say this country will eat you — piece by piece.   It likes to savor each bone.

It likes to play with our bodies like cats before they kill the mouse.

> Occasionally, she would change it up and say that the coyote kissed her.
> We would laugh and ask my father if he was going to beat up the coyote.

> He'd say, *with this bad knee, the coyote would out-run him.*

He too had given of his body.   He too   had sinned.

On My Parent's Cuadra

There's a lady who is skinny from diabetes but still eats pan dulce y galletas daily. My mother says she is a hardhead because she won't listen to the doctor to stop eating so much sugar. My mom likes the skinny lady because she knows how to carry on a conversation. My mother still asks me to buy her soda from the grocery store. She, too, is diabetic.

There's Rene, who is in a coma after falling from his chair; he is the cuadra's drunk. Three ladies, including my mother, give him beans and tortillas every now and then. My mother doesn't see it as enabling. She sees it as community taking care of their own. She prays for him.

There's La Carnicera, who is angry at the local government for closing businesses due to the pandemic. My mother only buys half of what she intends to purchase. She doesn't want to reward bad energy.

There's the guy who sells Birria de Chivo — and has been doing so for the last 18 years — on the same corner, under the same tree, at the same time every day except when it rains.

My mother says that when she leaves this country, *for good,* she will sell posole, sopes and tostadas twice a week, para no enfadarme, mijo.

This time, there are five deaths on my parent's cuadra: el niño que se ahogó, la mamá del cerrajero, el carpintero, la esposa del primo de tú papa, y el 'Don' de la tienda. I ask my mother if she knows their names. She doesn't know all of them personally, *but they were part of the community, and that's what we do,* she explained.

And that's what we do.

May God have mercy on them, and may their families not suffer so much, she says.

    May God have mercy. That's what we do.

My Grandmother Has Ethiopian Food for the First Time

She seems uneasy at how the lentils,
carrots, potatoes, spinach,
chicken, beef, and the salad
are served on a big tin plate
on top of the anjera.

¿Y los tenedores? she whispers,
wanting to avoid getting the waiter in trouble.

The waiter, who is the owner of the restaurant,
must have understood, brought a plate
and a fork and placed it
next to my grandmother.

He proceeded to explain that
eating like this was how it was before colonization.
None divided. All together. Now, I want fork,
I want plate. Mine! Mine!

I translated what he said to my grandmother,
and she attempts to eat with her hands,
giggles as she puts food into her mouth.

I have seen my grandmother laugh and cry many times.
I rarely hear her giggle. So, I forgive her for eating
with a fork and using her own plate.

A giggle is enough
to not worry about colonization for the day.

When Returning from Mexico

My mother and father always say, *next year.*
We will finish building our house next year.

After 25 years of working on it,
they only need the walls painted.

Next year, we will get it done, vieja.
Next year, we will paint the walls, viejo.

Next year, they plan on
planting more fruit trees,

pruning the old ones, eating more mangos
and spending the rainy season in Mexico.

My father misses the sound of rain
and crack of thunder. His face

lights up when he talks about *next year.*
My mother stares into the piece of cheese

in the middle of the table while we
eat and gossip. *Next year,* she says,

I'll eat more cheese when I am down there.
Next year, my father says, I am done with this country.

Next year, he wants to plant rows of corn under a parota tree.
Next year, my mother wants to sell posole in her cuadra.

Next year. That's how we live. Always planning one step
at a time. The future is never promised to people

like us. *Next year, who knows who will live,*
my mother reminds us, *but if we are alive*

let's do more — next year. Let's enjoy more
next year.
Next year.   Next year.

The Evening After We Buried My Father

My grandmother suggested that I set my alarm early. *The trash needs to be out in the corner by six in the morning*, she says.

/ /

The alarm sounds at 5:30 a.m. I listen for my father's footsteps. I wiggle my toes. I run my hands over the bed sheets toward my lover's body. I bend my knees and take a deep breath. I know soon a part of my body will be a ghost.

/ /

I awake startled. My cell phone shines at 5:57 a.m. on my face. I jump out of bed rush to the back patio, and pick up the bag full of trash. It is surprisingly light; it smells of rotten meat and coffee. I sleepily balance atop the cobblestone street towards the corner. I notice the red brakes of a big truck a few blocks down.

I stand in the middle of the street, pondering if I want to run with the trash bag to try to catch the truck.

A man silently walks in my direction. ¿Oiga, ya paso la basura? I ask. No, he responds. ¿Y a qué horas pasa? I toss the words at him, hoping his words will save me from my family's ridicule after sleeping through my alarm. He smiles at me. "Pues, como a las siete," he says without breaking a stride and disappears into the dark. I am not one to believe strangers, so I ask the second man walking towards me, ¿Oiga, a que horas pasa la basura? "Como a las ocho," he says and disappears into the dark just like the man before him did.

Standing in the corner, shivering and holding the trash bag, resentment grows toward my grandmother. But she didn't raise no fool. So, when a third man walks by, I ask, ¿A que horas pasa la basura? He stops, briefly looks around. "Pues como a las nueve... esa no tiene hora." His tone borders on sarcasm, as if I should know this information already, but I don't, and apparently, neither did my grandmother. He disappears into the same dark as the two men before him did.

/ /

I finish telling this story next to the table where my father had his last beer. My family explodes in laughter. My grandmother makes excuses, my aunt howls at the ceiling, my mother smiles and shakes her head, my girlfriend's face reddens from giggling, thunder comes from my brother's chest, and no part of my body feels like a ghost.

> In unison, we all catch our breath,
> and head over to the next room
> to start my father's rosary.

Bodies

I get off the phone, and I am frustrated with my mother.
She is in Mexico. We talked about the virus while she
peeled a papaya to eat. She thanked me for the payment
I made to her job so that she would not lose her benefits
for being away. If she were truly essential, maybe my money
would not be necessary.

> I am frustrated by her loyalty to her job, which pays
> her enough to have breathing room, but with every
> paycheck, there seems to be one more bill that needs to
> wait to be paid next month or the month after. *We have*
> *to be thankful,* she says. I am frustrated because of what
> loyal servants capitalism makes of us all. I tell my mother,
> *You have hypertension,*

diabetes, arthritis, you limp when you get to work, and still, you want to pay them? I
am frustrated by how good of a worker she is. I am frustrated by how, for many of
us, pride comes before our own dignity. I hate how we are made to believe that if we
work hard enough, if we do not bite the hand that feeds us, we will prosper. I hate
how this country has broken down my mother's body.

> *It is not about the money, Mom,* I say. *You should be able*
> *to eat papayas every day without having to worry about*
> *insurance co-pays or if your arthritis will let you work*
> *pain-free.* She reminds me she's not lazy. She is right.
> She is not. She is stubborn. She laughs when I tell her
> this.

Before the factory job, she was a farm worker. She picked many
harvest seasons into the pockets of banks and landowners, and they
praised her for the way she broke her back. We jealously looked
at the landowner's children when they went on ski trips, while we scratched
our heads when the bank charged us interest for cashing
our checks. Once, while helping my mother pick harvest seasons
into the pockets of others, I worked alongside a thin-wrinkly

> brown man. He was seventy but managed to work in
> the fields. *This is the life that was meant for us,* he added
> while limping away, making his way up the aluminum
> ladder to pick more fruit from the tree. It saddens me
> that he, like my mother, thinks that their broken-down
> bodies are payment for being able to breathe   [in]
> this country.

Conversations I'd Like to Have With My Mother

The day you decided not to take my biological father back — did you listen to music? If so, what song?

When he asked you to abort me — how did it change you?
                              Tell me about the first boy you ever loved.

If there was a time machine — where AND what period would you travel to?
                              What would you wear for the occasion?

What was more complicated: crossing the border alone   or   leaving me behind?
What was moree complicated: getting deported   or   not being present
                                                    at your father's funeral?

                    Tell me about his hands.

What was the first song you knew by heart?

                    Please, can you sing it?

You were holding Abuela Esperanza's hand when she took her last breath?
                    How long did you wait before washing your hands?

What did she say to you before she died?
                    If you could cook one last meal for her, what would it be?
                    Where would you eat it?

While eating omelets by the train station, you told me you learned to love my stepfather. Do you remember the day you fell in love with him?
                    What was the weather like that day?

Tell me about the first time you saw him cry. Tell me about the last time.

You also mentioned your depression. I told you about mine and how scary it can be.
                    How do you cope?

Where are my sisters buried? Do you dream of them?
                    What were you going to name them?

What is your favorite flower? What is your favorite season?

¿Cuándo me vas a enseñar a bordar?

Tell me about the first time you danced all night. Who is your favorite musician?

If this country was a song — what song would it be?

What is making you smile today?

For the days we need to be gentle with ourselves

Ode to 1990s Banda

Before I heard the slogan "Brown is Beautiful" Banda Machos
reminded me *que la sangre de indio que traigo es mejor* and to be aware of
culebras. They were ahead of their time, telling us
to be proud of our indigenous roots, to watch out for people
coming to mess with our spirit. They were like the Zapatistas but
instead of ski masks, they wore boots and spurs, and made us dance!

Under the lemon tree, my auntie cut my hair. Six-year-old me
told her to cut from the top pero dejeme una cola. I wanted
to rock my tejana with a mullet peeking from underneath my
cowboy hat like Raul, the lead singer from Banda Machos.
I wanted to walk this world with the same audacity of a mullet.

Ernesto, from Banda Maguey, was short, dark, and handsome.
When he jumped on stage with his arms up in the air, he brought smiles
to our faces. His feet landed on the floor with such conviction,
we had no choice but to be joyful, too. He sang about sugarcane
fields, beaches, and being eternally in love. He made me believe
there was no difference between loving someone or a place.

My auntie cut my mullet off, stating that it was not authentic,
that I would not get respect in society; I would be
perceived as vulgar and uneducated. I heard the wind make
music with the leaves of the lemon tree. I confused my hair
with a lemon being shaken off from
the tree. I thought the tree was crying, but it was me.

Ode to the brass instruments that held my spirit when
my branches seemed empty of blossoms. Ode to
the singer and the backup dancers, swirling and twisting
with the courage of a machete against an army of canons
coming to take our smiles away. Ode to the weaponizing of
our footsteps. Ode to the crowd in the bailes chanting and singing.

Me siento muy contento
Hoy es fin de semana y
El viernes me desvelo y
Y el domingo me enredo
Feliz feliz, feliz feliz

me siento muy feliz
me pienso divertir
el sábado también
con quien me quiera bien
feliz feliz, feliz feliz

For Brown Boys Who Want to Believe We Are Beautiful (or Letter to Myself)

Whenever your lungs feel unworthy of harboring the quiver of your breath, know your lineage is molded by hands whose only purpose in life has been to provide you with the right to breathe.

Inhale
deep and soft.

Whenever your heart feels untouched and your stomach feels empty of butterflies, whenever you curse your body for not being big enough to hurt, whenever you curse your body for being too small to let yourself be hurt, whenever you curse your body for not being able to undo wrongs, whenever you curse your body for destroying, for pillaging and conquering, for being trapped and burning, know that no sorrow is everlasting.

There's no dirt heavy enough
to keep a seed from sprouting;
There's no winter long enough
to keep the spring from coming.

Be patient with yourself, Brown boy,
    You— boundless forest waiting to be explored.
    You— bouquet of flowers on a first date.
    You— oasis in the middle of the barrio.
    You— beautiful Sunday morning church.
    You— beautiful choir of holy hymns.
    You— answered prayer.
    You— unneeding of God to believe in your sacredness.

Be gentle with yourself, Brown boy,
    and know
    there are waves ready to rest upon the shores
    of your forgiveness. Know stardust cannot be shackled.
    Know that in the longest of nights, in the most infinite dark,
    there will still be instruments.
            And know,
        somewhere out there, there's a room full of eager dancers
        waiting for you
            to sing.

It is May

Spring is my favorite season. For the last years
I was convinced it was fall and its colors. Today I sat

next to a river, and I was sure that if I placed my cheek
ground level—opened my mouth—the river would

disappear into my body. I imagined fresh-water trout
eating the cavities logged in my wisdom teeth

and salmon swimming to my feet, staying until they'd return
to my throat where they'd lay their eggs. It is May, and I cried

today for the first time in months. I did not feel alone. I think
the breeze and therapy had something to do with it. I do not

remember the first time I skipped a stone across water. I am
trying to remember the colors of the trees in the fall.

I do not remember the many shades of green there are or
if the rapids I stared at—while trying to swallow the river—

always sound like laughter. Honestly, I do not see a difference
between spring and fall. In one, you are shedding the old;

in the other, the new is flowering. The birds sing in both seasons—
a sad song because they are leaving, a happy song

because they are returning. I am not sure I can
swallow a river or if my skin would make a good shoreline.

If sprouting out of ashes is always this pleasant, let me emerge
out of the ground like a thousand fireflies in May.

Hummingbirds

The Mayans noticed that when the Gods were done
Creating trees, animals, rivers, rocks,
Humans, wind, and the sun, there
Was no means to carry messages between
Living beings. So, out of a piece of jade, they
Crafted the hummingbird. Its wings are delicate enough to
Kiss and caress a flower yet strong enough to fly
Swiftly and far. The purpose of the hummingbird is freedom.
When you see one, it is believed that someone,
Living or not, is sending you a message.

/ /

I bought my father a sunflower plant for Father's Day.
I plan to give one to my brother, too. I am gifting
Them flowers because I forget to call. My hope is that
They will water them, tend to them like they tended
To this heart of mine, teaching me that
These hands were meant to be free.
I am moving away from them—again.
But I think of them always. My wish is for a hummingbird
To carry my forgetfulness and deliver it to them.

/ /

I saw a hummingbird while writing this today. It had red
Wings. It kissed the flowers next to me before flying
Swiftly away. Red. Maybe it was my grandfather's messenger.
Red. He fought for this land. Red. He might have been murdered
For it. Red. I whispered a prayer to the hummingbird. Red. I blew
A kiss at it, too. Red. Can a hummingbird carry touch as well?

/ /

I met my biological father eight years ago.
I gave him my phone number and email to reach out
Whenever he wanted to talk. I am told we are the same.
I carry many of his traits. Maybe he thinks of me
But forgets to call. I wish I would have known about
The hummingbirds back then. I could have told him about them.
We could have gifted each other flowers.

My Father the Horse

I thought there would be closure after meeting my biological father.

I imagined a small, colorful bird flapping its wings
inside my chest, its feathers turning into tears
and my arms—perfect arcs of rainbows after a storm—
hugged him as I whispered that I missed him.
                              But it never happened.
I have no memories of him.

                    Just mannerisms my mother said
                    I inherited from him. Like the way
                    I stutter when I get nervous.

I was told he liked to ride horses; he had many to choose from.

As a kid, I thought any unfamiliar man riding a horse into our town
during las fiestas could be my father. I would mingle among the strangers,
resting on the back of their horses, listening for a thin brown man's stutter.
My ears could never differentiate between the human voice and the sound
of a horse's hooves landing on the ground.

Maybe my father was a horse—dark-maned with a long-braided tail. He'd have
brown hair, the kind that looks red from one angle and mahogany from another.
Maybe his lower legs were black, and he'd look like he was floating when he walked.
His mouth would also be black; he'd smile, happy to graze upon green fields.

Maybe his eyes would be deep, making me feel like I could touch the bottom of an abyss.
I would ride on his back across the papaya field, down the canyon into the river. He
would neigh after gulping water, and I'd run my hand down his back, feeling the
length of his spine, his smooth body would shiver.

>   There's a dream—my mother's.
>   She carries a baby's body in her arms,
>   wandering in some town at night.
>   Everybody closes their windows when she passes
>   by weeping and hollering. She never meant
>   for the baby to perish. She would've done anything
>   to save the child, but the baby appeared
>   in her arms like grief suddenly surfaces.

A man stands in front of her, yelling angrily,
if I had stayed here, and my mother weeps
louder, offers the baby to the man, who stutters
when he tries to talk to the lifeless baby.
The man is angry, not sad, and my mother
is ashamed and full of guilt.

I must've been in my early twenties when my mother
told me about her dream. She asked me to fly to Mexico
to meet my biological father.

I do not remember where I was or how I responded.
I remember my heart clawing my mouth open,
I remember my mother's tears rolling down her face,
staring into space. When I glanced at the spot where
she was looking at, I saw nothing.
       Maybe she was imagining my dead body,
       or the stuttering man yelling at her.

My father looked nothing like the horse I imagined
when I met him.

He is light-skinned and claims to come
from people who never left the mountains.
I sensed pride when he shared that.

He has a potbelly, and I am a bit taller
than him. He stutters when he is nervous
and, like me, he repeats himself when his thoughts
are unclear. When we shook hands, I wondered if he
felt the bird in my chest when our palms met. I did
not give my arms to become rainbows. I was
not mad or resentful. I assumed that if
I opened the door to the cage, which I did,
the bird would fly away, but it did not. It is
still in here. I did not stutter
when I talked to him. I'm still trying

to figure out why and what it means.

I do not recall his eyes or the sound of his voice.
We sat next to each other, looking straight
at the white wall in front of us. I remember
his left ear. Its edges looked soft and red. I
wanted to touch my ear and hold his at the same
time. He had a red neck from being out in the sun.
He smelled of cows. I wanted to tell him about
my greatest regret—leaving my town. Instead,
I asked him how many cows he owned.
I can't remember what he said—three, four.
I was distracted by how he rubbed his ears
when he spoke.
                        Just like me.

He kept looking at his hands. Maybe he had
the same dream as my mother,
                              or maybe he
was waiting for his bird to fly away;
maybe he was waiting   for his hands
                    to turn into
            rainbows.

Hands Before and After Burial

¡Salte, cabron, no es tuyo! My uncle scolds me for getting
into the plastic toy car parked next to the stove. He bends
down to pick my 8-year-old body up in his arms—he smiles,
kisses my cheek, and sets me on the floor. I notice his gold
necklace, the one with a tiny crucifix, resting on his breastbone.
His shirt isn't buttoned up all the way—just like the picture
I saw of him before I met him. He smells good.
I would find his cologne stash when I got older—BRUT,
his favorite. I hug his waist and bury
my embarrassment into his hip. He places his left
hand on my shoulders and holds me gently.

In the picture, my uncle, still in Mexico,
stands with his friends at a street
corner of our small town. He was 15,
my grandmother informed me. I have
no memories of this uncle until we
are in the kitchen. In the picture, he looks
sharp, good-looking, dark, stoic, with soft, thin
lips. Hands full of veins. Slicked-back hair.
A smile that has not yet buried his father.
His posture is relaxed, and he looks
straight into the camera. His eyes—two
pieces of black jade—sparkle without
death. Those are the prettiest eyes—the
ones with no dead bodies in them.

In the kitchen, his hands have already shoveled dirt onto
his father's casket. They have already hammered the cross
to his grave. He has already washed the dry blood from them.
His mouth has already wept loudly. His eyes have cried so much
they've puffed up red. His hands are smooth as I explore them
with mine. His voice is soothing and sure of itself. The black jades
shimmer when he laughs, sending a shiver of joy down my spine.
They say a part of you is buried with the loved one in the casket.
I wondered if his hands were softer before the burial.

As I stared at him, I wondered which part of this
miraculous brown body embracing me is incomplete?

I Cry With My Uncles

We are leaning on the white truck facing intó its bed
I say something about trust
They something about having my back

I say something about feeling like an ocean or a beach
How sometimes it is calm, sometimes rough with waves
They nod in understanding

One of them says something that breaks me
I stay silent
                                They embrace me

They each whisper in my ear how much they love me
I can hear   and feel
                                                their tears

When they kiss my shoulders in their attempts to console me
When their rough hands wipe my tears
It feels like I am walking in a meadow, picking a bouquet of flowers.

For Brown Boys Who Want to Love Themselves (or Another Letter to Myself)

Es un poquito complicado
Tener al diablo aquí a mi lado
Le dije que se fuera y no se quiere ir
Al parecer el sol otra vez va a salir

— Gera MX, *"Complicado"*

There will be days, brown boy,
when the warmth of someone's arms
will feel undeserving
and empty. Days when it might
seem better to turn into ash.

In a room full of ghosts and bones of someone you used to know,
you will practice your smile for someone's benefit, and
you will feel like uncaging white doves into the sky, as if the war
was won. You will keep practicing that smile
until there are tears roll down her face,
and she will knock on the door to ask if everything is okay.
You will be relieved you are not the one crying,
you will feel pride for this.

There will be days
when phrases like *love yourself*
will seem like you are diving head-first
out of an airplane onto the valley below,
and the parachute on your back will not open.

On days like these—

it will become apparent
why they clipped our wings when they made us believe
that boys like us—
                    we don't cry.
We blame and maim,
break and tear, slash and burn—
you uncontrolled fire, you!

There will be days
when every word, every action you have taken
to dehumanize and use someone
will come back to sit on your chest,
                            suffocating you.
On days like these, you will comprehend the weight of words.
How metaphors—a mountain for a throat,
a mouth full of arrows—are not really metaphors.

There will be days
when looking into yourself will scare you.
Days when the illusion of being invincible will crumble.
Days when you must admit that you are not strong enough.
Days when it will be okay to let your facade shrivel into dust.
      Days when you will need to ask for help to patch yourself
                                  back together with the pieces
                                  worth saving from the rubble.

This is what it means to love ourselves.

This is what it looks like to let go of our demons—

                        Please,   let them go;
                                        stop hugging them so tight.

                        There are other ways of being loved.

                        And please,

                        stop smiling like

                                it's really beginning

                                        to scare me.

Soft Hurt

Yesterday I dreamed a rat clawed my hand.

I was drinking tea with my mother, father, and brother.

We were all sitting in a bed I used to sleep in.
I was covered with a blanket.

My father looked young.
My mother was radiant.
My brother's laugh was deep and loud.
Dusk rested perfectly on their faces.

I was the only one that noticed the rat.
        I did not feel any pain when it clawed me.
        I didn't even flinch.

I am confused because today
        I cried when I merged on the highway,
            Then again when I saw the clouds,
                Then again when I sang in the car,
                    Then again when I was silent.

        I am confused because the softest things

        seem to hurt the most.

Marbles

We played marbles underneath the branches of the almond tree while the birds sang. If your marble was hit out of the square of play or if it was hit more than a spread-palm's length away from its original spot, you gave that marble to the player who hit it. You could play the game with as many marbles as was agreed upon beforehand. We would also bet an X number of marbles per game. We would play like this under the almond tree until the top of our thumb would be tender from using it as a trigger to shoot our marble into other marbles. When one of us wanted to quit before all our marbles were pushed out or hit far away, we would hold out our thumb for the other players to examine. If it was decided that it was not tender enough—by how it looked or by how it felt or by the lack of blood—one would still have to play. This is the masculinity I used to know: boys caressing each other's hands making sure that we were not too hurt to stop listening to the birds sing.

Wishing Well

my body feels like a mine today—
            gold or coal

                                    I don't know
            what rests in me these days.
                    it is dark in this mine of mine.
today,
                I scare myself.
the same way an ocean scares me
for it can absorb me into itself
and no one will confuse me for
a buoy   or a fish.

who will light the lighthouse at the shore if I lose myself into myself?

today, I am peeping into my mouth as if it was the edge of a wishing well.

I yell into myself   into the mouth of my well   and echoes crawl
down my throat   until   they are distant
                                                                 and quiet.

I wait for the shrill of bats, but it is quiet and lonely
inside the well of my mouth.   for a moment

I want to propel myself into myself,
roped with a sturdy rope around my waist,
with the meat of a ripe mango as my lantern.

I want to dust the walls of myself with the petals of a sunflower,
expose what is beneath the bones.
I want to see if history does, in fact, repeat itself.

I did not know becoming this enormous
would make me feel so small. I did not how the glow of the
moon hanging from the sky inside my body would feel like a black hole.
maybe all this dark.   all this dancing with no movement
is hope   I have yet   to discover, and I am waiting
on myself   to throw a coin   into my mouth.

Untitled

After Anis Mojgani

In this chest, there is a clock. Somedays, I am late for who I want to become. Other days, I am early, and depending on the weather, I find myself somewhere on some path, captivated by how the wind moves through the leaves and how the branches sway, crackling to make music. In this chest of mine, there is also a tiny lightbulb. I flick the switch and become a lighthouse. I am looking for a place to rest so someone can find a home. I sit in front of the mirror.

/ /

I can see smoke from afar. I know there are flames somewhere, but I cannot see them. I drive into this wildfire, singing a song about a sea. The song says something about letting go. The guitar is sharp, and the voice singing is that of a young girl. The song says something about stars. Something about kissing and starting over. I can't see my smoke, but I know there are flames somewhere. I tried to find them while breaking down on the couch today. I wish I could kiss all of this away.

/ /

I don't need to be near you. I just want to hear your voice. Said my mother's mouth to my father's mouth. Said our teenage hearts, learning to fall in love. Said fans of Nipsey and Amy Winehouse. Said my mouth, calling from a basement in Laramie, Wyoming.

/ /

The horse stopped running once it felt the rope on its mane. This would happen, my uncle had said. *You won't need to get the rope around its neck*, were his exact words. Circus elephants, as babies, are shackled to heavy metal chains that are impossible to break. Once adults, elephants can easily break these chains but decide not to.

//

I've grown comfortable in this bed of nails I sleep upon. I've learned to distribute my weight evenly to keep the nails from puncturing my skin. I know there are softer things to sleep on. I know there are delicate parts of me that I've yet to touch for fear of losing the safety these nails provide.

/ /

Violins are playing in my chest. There is a dance floor on my stomach. She taps her fingers on my belly button and waltzes over my goose-bumped skin. There is a topography I wish to feel, the braille of the lover I want to hold tonight.

//

There is a lamp in this room. There is a butterfly on a hat. There is a flower on someone's shoulder. There is a stream, waterfall, planets, stars, and mirrors. Somewhere there is a universe where holding hands is a river arriving at the ocean, a salmon swimming back to its birthplace, and there—wherever this place is—be the warmest and easiest of mornings.

//

Saturday morning comes like most others, with the sun peeking over the horizon, trying to catch a glimpse of the moon, and in her arms I wake. There are things that I cherish more than the sun—the way she says *hi* at first light. The way our feet touch under the bedsheets, the way her chest rises like the breathing of a forest, the way she wraps her arm around me and asks, *how was your sleep?*

//

I am walking and planting flowers. I am turning stones and flipping rocks and tossing a hat on my head. The sun is building a nest on my shoulders, and I have always wanted wings. There is a river that I once knew, rapids I once heard, a shoreline I once stood upon where I tried to skip rocks onto the shoreline across. There is a book I wish to read, and there is a song I want to sing the words to without stumbling, without losing a beat, hitting every note just like the sunlight lands on my lover's skin.

//

I am not that good at love poems. I am not that good at love either. But most days, regardless of time or weather, I am good at arriving and trying.

Artist Statement

My body of work is much like an ocean.   It scares me
                              my body for   how loud
and destructive   it can be when it wants something   or someone.

I am learning to use form and structure. Often, I employ memory as a means to an end. Really, really though, I have no sense of form or structure. I say things to sound like I know what I am talking about. You should know that I am Mexican; hence, my relationship with borders is complicated at best.

In bed most mornings, I wonder what my grandmother is doing. I think of the last time I heard her laugh. It is getting distant   her laugh.

The work in my body is a storm approaching, and I purposely do not board the windows.

I cannot remember when I learned to swim, but when I was a boy, I tried to run across the beach, and the sand was hot. I stood there yelling for help, and my grandmother picked me up and carried me away. I swam all afternoon, blisters forming at the bottom of my feet. I remember her laugh then.

My poems are about me as a little boy—you can say it is inner-child work, but I prefer to say—memory.

I write poems because I never could become a bull rider. By that, I mean I am brave in these poems,   and I do not care who sees me fall. Even when I fall, the crowd's cheers, and that makes this [body of] work more manageable.

Sing Me a Brown Song

After Nikki Giovanni

Sing me a Brown song until your mouth breathes fire like a sweat lodge until it is known that the singular of tamales is tamal;

Sing it until we claim Spanish and English as our second, third, fourth, fifth, sixth, seventh, or eighth language. We've existed since before there was a word for tongue;

Sing me a Brown song until we stop calling ourselves hispanic; Until we—
Latino Latina Latin@ Latinx Latine Chicana Chicano Chicanx
Charrua Chapin Chapulin Chichas Chicharitos Cholas Chulas
Chingonas Cabronas Chilangos Chalinos Chismosos Catrachos
Cafeteros Canaleros Colimenses Costeños Caribeños Cajeños
Oaxaquenos Norteños Sureños Trokiando Cheds Tlacuaches Cuhs
Brujos Brujas Brújulas y Burbujas Nicas Nicos Niñas Niños
Guarinis Jibaros Guanaços Salvis Ticos Ticas Tacos de Tripas Rudos
y Rudas Rudos y Cursis Fresas y Cerezas Selenas y Selenos Mojados
Chopas Truchas y Pescados Moreno Morenito Malinche Mechista
Machista El Apache Light-skinned White-Passing Indigenous-Mestizos
Wannabe indios Pochos Paisas Prietos Negros Brown Bag Test
AANNDDD! no sabo kids

Agree on one singular unifying term for all of us.

Sing me a Brown song on your caballo
in your troca   in your impala
in your botas   in your cortezes
in your huaraches   in your danza Azteca

Sing me a Brown song until the smell of copal surpasses the scent of patchouli
for the hippy-est shit ever;

Sing it until my homies start accepting credit cards at the healing ceremonies;

Sing me a Brown song until "El Chico del Apartamento 512" gets a house with a yard y la querida de Juan Gabriel returns, and your heartbreak becomes a wood stove in the middle of winter, and we learn to tame the wildfires with our bedsheets when we become firefighters for the sole reason that we like to carry water in our hands. We learn how to juggle hot charcoals like we do our insecurities, and we kiss each other like volcano-smoke kisses the sky when we fall into each other's palms like our torso's fall into each other after climax;

Sing me a Brown song until la Llorona finds her children and absentee fathers stop playing the longest games of hide and seek;

Sing it until ICE melts into water, and we plant gardens on the rubble of detention centers, make swing sets out of its metal and steel, and we play wall ball and graffiti its walls, make windchimes and chandeliers out of melted guns, hearing them howl like a hanging purgatory;

Sing me a Brown song with pianos and violins and tubas and guitars and trumpets and drums and accordions and saxophones and a tololoche and a bajo sexto and our loved ones' laughter;

Sing it with all the prayers left on the street corners. Sing it until the candles at funerals burn because our loved ones have risen and are returning with jars full of tears that turned into honey wine;

Sing it until *rosary*   becomes the word

        we use

for story-time about flowers.

Alameda Avenue

For Oscar & for all the students we've lost
After Langston Hughes

There—on Alameda Avenue—where Little Mexico begins.
There—the place their bulldozer's teeth are salivating for,
where paleteros honk a horn, children come running
like bees to pollinate a flower, and their smiles are honey,
and a springtime grows in their baby-fat-filled hands.
This—the place for Sunday morning church and Sunday night cruising.
All joy in these streets. Potholes are a reminder to slow down and enjoy
the blue and pink sky on a summer night.
Truck burnouts to amplify laughter; Corridos to speak happiness
in more than one language, botas to stay rooted; Tejana to prove
they are Mexican while they eat a bowl of Pho. Shit-talking morros
y morras asking where the plug be; when the race to Lookout be;
  where will the cops be hiding, B?
  Be happy here, be eternal here.
  This place will remember you,
  Brown boy.

There—on Alameda Avenue—in front of St. Cajetan's Church, Oscar took
his last breath while trying to tame the wind like he tamed those horses.
There—a vigil of brown faces, all lit with burial in their eyes.
There—Jesús cried, and Cesar, too. And Darwin, Raul, Daniel, Carlos, Exar, Erick,
Rene, Ernesto, and me—we all cried. And there were not enough
candles to melt our sadness onto the pavement.
We tried praying, but we hugged each other instead.
We were a choir of weeping brown boys. How beautiful to sing
like that. How ceremonial to hold each other like that.
I will never agree with how these streets give us back to the earth.
But we were there, holding each other like the sky holds its night.
One of our stars fell that evening,
  landed on our cheeks,
  made singers out of us.
  O, how we howled into
  each other's chests that night.

There—on Alameda Avenue—inside of St. Cajetan's Church, the casket held his
body. Gently tucked within layers of shiny, pearl white cloth, dressed in clothes
picked by his mother. His eyes looked as if they wanted to open.

His lips—a horse's neigh silenced. The mariachi sang sad songs.
The guitars did not make us want to dance. The trumpets tried
but could not drown out his mother's cry. The singer of sad songs
took a seat and let the sobs in the room be accompanied by instruments.
This ritual of letting go, this practice of parents outliving their children,
this sore throat, this emptiness, these dry eyes death leaves us with is something
I will never embrace. The priest said Oscar is in a better place now. I looked
at his mother's arms but they were empty. I looked at his girlfriend's lips and they
were not being kissed by his.
If after this, it is better to let him be laughing,
                    let him be riding his favorite horse
                    down Alameda Avenue.
                    Let him stay happy like he is now.
                    Please, let him stay happy like that.

What We Ask of Eyes

He said he'd only give me a warning.
This, only after he listened to my poetry
And he liked how deep it was
How they called me beaner.
He asked me not to speed on my way down the mountain.

Before all of this, he asked where I was coming from.
             A show.
      You're a musician?
             No, a reading I meant.
      You're a card reader?
             No, I am a poet.
    Oh, is your stuff online?
             Yes.

Before all that, he asked if I knew I was speeding.

Oh no, I was passing a car, sir, I am sorry, sir.
Do you want my license, sir? Okay, here you go, sir.

Before all of this,
I prayed softly
Kept my hands on the steering wheel,
Reminding myself that my mother is the beneficiary on my bank accounts,
Reminding myself, I told my friend that I too would want Banda all night
At my funeral.

You better not fucking cry! she had said.

I didn't promise anything.

I couldn't remember what I asked of her eyes.

Death in Cuyutlán

After Danez Smith

i. the ocean

the sun was setting, & the reflection of its rays was being juggled by the waves—
back & forth, back & forth. my cousins & i bathed in dusk-gold waters, walked
onto the shoreline, laughing like we've never known silence. i don't remember
pain when my lips stretch past the ends of my mouth. the sand was soft-brown
color & the grains felt like tiny, prickly stars trying to reunite with the stardust in
my bones. we looked out to the horizon—past where the waves began to rise—&
saw him floating, mouth pointed towards heaven as if wanting to return his
stardust to the sky.

> *he's really way out there, huh?* my cousin asks.
>
> *i know, he must be a good swimmer.*

ii. the body

i thought he was back-stroking
 chest above the water like a buoy signaling—*too deep*;
head tilted back, mouth opened as if accepting
 sunset as the body of Christ;
shoulders—two mounds of earth rising from the sea-bed—
 looked like a pile of delicate brown rose petals gliding on the surface.
all the beachgoers in Cuyutlán were pointing
 at the brown body floating parallel to the horizon.
we all gawked at his effortlessness to wade in the ocean;
 the ocean seemed to embrace him,
and i was amazed at how its arms cradled him
 like a newborn being passed from one family member's arms to the next.
i wondered what his skin might feel like,
 maybe his hands would remind me of my uncle's.
perhaps he was a farmworker
 who loved to cook or play an instrument.
i wanted his serenity and peace
 like a storm before it makes everybody hide.
i wanted my body to make the ocean seem small and insignificant.

iii. drowned

that's how you died that afternoon.
when the waves pushed you onto the beach
& people flocked around you like seagulls,
some screamed & some asked your name.   *[what is your name?]*
when the teenager ran towards us screaming, ¡se ahogo! ¡se ahogo!
i imagined a starfish making a home out of your stomach,
i imagined a whale swimming in & out of your heart's arteries,
i imagined an octopus crawling on the floor of your veins,
i imagined a coral reef forming in the backside of your ribcage,
i imagined fish eating plankton from your femurs,
& seaweed braiding itself with each of your vertebrae.
how ceremonial to flourish upon death,
how proper to witness a life ending and starting all at once,
how beautiful it must be to die like that.

/ /

i want my death beautiful, like that.
in front of everybody so no one goes looking for my body,
so that every time my mother looks at the ocean, wherever
she is, she sees part of me. any time she wants to find me,
she can just follow a river & if she wants to feel my embrace,
she can dip her feet into the water. the crashing waves
will be my laughter & she will not wonder how i died.
she will be content knowing that each wave hugged me like a newborn
& when the waves cradled me in their arms,
they reminisced about an ancestor that i reminded them of;
in my smile, they'd see all of my possibilities.
my mother will not have to post missing pictures of me,
she will not have to convince witnesses to come forward.
when we found him, she'd say, *his body was entirely of nature.*

/ /

a body filled with nature when found instead of
bullets, isn't that what we all deserve?
when i leave here, i want to be
open-mouthed swallowing life back into my body as
i choke on the mountains crumbling onto my tongue,

as i choke on the birds and their feathers,
as i choke on grasslands, my liver becomes
a red mango tree, my heart becomes a moon
to signal the start of planting season, & bees pollinate flowers
growing from my intestines
my blood will be replaced by fresh water cascading from my esophagus
into the valley of my lungs. i want to die like this—
Mother Nature coming to ask for me,
come back inside. it's dark already. dinner is served
come eat before it gets cold.

      / /

before we realized your body was cold—
my cousins & i sat in our chairs & marveled
at how radiant your skin looked, drifting like a cloud
before our eyes. we called you—a good swimmer.
we called you—brave. we called you every superhero
we could think of, & you saved the day & captured
every villain. we named you everything except—murdered, missing,
dismembered—pieces of body in black plastic bags left on roadsides.
your resting place will not be a clandestine grave in the mountains.
your resting place will not be a desert, & the sun will not eat at you slowly.
your whole body will be present at your funeral.
we witnessed your death today, & that's a holy sacrament.
in your open casket, your mother will caress your skin
& that gives me hope for my death.

      / /

i hope to outlive my mother
& my death is not like in the dreams i dream
where i am in a gold casket
& a candle burns, where my mother becomes ash
from all the praying & she doesn't
rise from the pain. her wings fly
the opposite of the sky. in another
dream there's a mariachi band
surrounding a silver casket &
i am singing a song my mother loved & my mother
loved & we are dancing, just as she asked,

& there's plenty of food, just how she liked,
& of death, we make a celebration

      / /

death made you a celebration.
made a community out of strangers,
all of us hoping you'd exhale again.
death made a siren scream & made a bystander
hug her children close, made swimmers
take a seat, made my cousin scared,
made me cry, made you a poem,
made everyone ask your name   *[what is your name?]*
made the paramedic feel your heart with his hands,
made the sun warm and our spines shiver,
made all the seagulls land and stop gawking,
made my cousin ask if you were no longer of this world.
you drank so much water,
your last breath sounded like waves.

      / /

you drank so much water your last breath sounded like a wave
where was the poem when the paramedics asked
for your family & there was no one to claim you? no one told us
your name. the paramedics would not know who to tell you
had become the ocean.

when the ambulance left with your body,
we sat and looked at the sun, dropping behind the water.
the waves were noiseless & empty of swimmers,
a gentle breeze somber as a howl & sand
blew into my eyes, reminded me of what
my grandmother had said about the stars when i was a boy,

they are all people who have died and are looking down, hoping
to see their loved ones.

i forgot to ask her how long after death before someone

                                becomes a star.

If the Brown body

dances or does not like to dance or does not know how to dance or is terrible at dancing; If the Brown body assimilates or wants a revolution or gains power, gets a seat at the table, if it is still denigrated and vilified or sells out or sells us out; If the Brown body lives a hyphenated existence, lives at the intersections, deviates from giving new meanings and creates and births new worlds; If the Brown body is femme or marimacha or gay lesbian trans- multi-spirit straight crooked pansexual asexual has no gender has no binary;

If the Brown body quivers before, during, or after orgasm or if it has never had an orgasm; If the Brown body denies itself or is fat or skinny from feasting on loving itself and from celebrating all the quinces, the 21st birthday parties, the births and first communions and from toasting with all the drunk tíos, and from dancing cumbia with all the aunties and from singing off key in the middle of the night; If the Brown body has no mother or homeland, and their father is a ghost; If the Brown body is raised by weathered hands, weary from pulling miracles out of thin air; If the Brown body is afraid to bury those hands or its own hands;

If the Brown body cries; If the Brown body suffers; If the Brown body calls itself a shrine; If the Brown body is not seen as worthy / is neglected / is deprived of light / of sage / of sweetgrass / of ceremony / becomes ill / spirit wanders / becomes / a picture on our altar / becomes / a memory we toast to with our tears / becomes / ash we swift through / in search of wings;

If the Brown body has no papers / exists where it is not wanted / speaks broken English / speaks broken [whatever language is their mother tongue] / is deported / is detained / is trafficked / is wronged / is silenced; If the Brown body disappears; If the Brown body reappears;

After we reemerge from these waters:

let us   mourn;
let us   grief;
let us   rejoice;
let us   create;
let us   try again;
let us   rebuild;
let us   rebuild;
let us   rebuild.

Acknowledgements

Thank you to the following editors where previous versions of these poems appeared:

The Acentos Review: "Alameda Street" "Hands Before and After Burial"
"Death in Cuyutlán"
The Santa Fe Reporter: "Poem About Immigration"
Publicintellectuals.org: "Dreams"

Thank you to my Tin House (2020) classmates for your insight into this manuscript before it was a manuscript.

Thank you, Jorge Quintana for your invaluable feedback on these poems in their very, very early stages.

Karla, thank you for your friendship and your comments and eyes on this book. Thank you for making feel less crazy and less alone. You are invaluable, Jita.

Anyel, THANK YOU for always believing in my work, even when I don't. Thank you for holding space. Thank you for your tenderness, your honesty, your love and grace. Thank you for celebrating, ecstatically, when I make tortillas y se inflan! And your laugh, thank you for that, too!

ALEJANDRO JIMENEZ is a nationally and internationally recognized poet from Colima, Mexico. He was featured in *TIME Magazine* as one of 80 Mexican artists shaping contemporary Mexican culture. His work, and story, are the subject of a short documentary for the PBS series, *American Masters: In The Making,* which highlights emerging cultural icons. He was runner-up at the 2023 World Poetry Slam Championships. He has been a high school counselor/student advisor for over a decade. He finds very few things to be better than laughing and writing with students.